PLEASE BRING BALLOONS

Lindsay Ward

Park Entrance SOUTH

ICE CREAM →

← GRAND CAROUSEL →

← exit

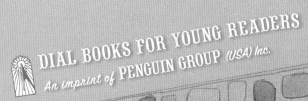

DIAL BOOKS FOR YOUNG READERS
An imprint of PENGUIN GROUP (USA) Inc.

For Frank, who always stands beside me
to watch the snow fall.

And for my Gramps, who loved to fly.

Dial Books for Young Readers
A division of Penguin Young Readers Group
Published by the Penguin Group
Penguin Group (USA) Inc., 375 Hudson Street, New York, New York 10014, USA

USA / Canada / UK / Ireland / Australia / New Zealand / India / South Africa / China
Penguin Books Ltd, Registered Offices: 80 Strand, London WC2R 0RL, England

For more information about the Penguin Group visit penguin.com

Copyright © 2013 by Lindsay Ward

Library of Congress Cataloging-in-Publication Data

Ward, Lindsay.
Please bring balloons / by Lindsay Ward.   p. cm.
Summary: Emma finds a note tucked into the saddle of a carousel polar bear
asking her to bring balloons, and soon she is off on an amazing adventure.
ISBN 978-0-8037-3878-2 (hardcover)
[1. Adventure and adventurers—Fiction. 2. Polar bear—Fiction.
3. Merry-go-round—Fiction.] I. Title.
PZ7.W214316Ple 2013 [E]—dc23   012033588

Manufactured in China on acid-free paper
10 9 8 7 6 5 4 3 2

Designed by Mina Chung • Text set in Colonial Dame

The publisher does not have any control over and does not assume
any responsibility for author or third-party websites or their content.

This art was created using cut paper, watercolor, and pencil.

It appeared unexpectedly.

Peeking out of the polar bear's saddle, a hint of paper.

Emma carefully folded the note into her pocket.

She'd never heard of polar bears writing notes or asking for balloons, but she decided to play along, just in case.

The next morning, Emma stopped by the
carousel on her way to school and tied a
single balloon to the polar bear's saddle.

"I hope you like red," she whispered.
And for just a second Emma thought
she saw him smile.

When Emma went back to the carousel that afternoon, the red balloon was still there . . .

with something tied to it.

Hmmm . . . she thought.
This must be important.

GAME 3

BOXES/K

BONUS

RETURN TO

After Emma had tied the last string, she hopped up onto the polar bear's saddle to wait.

At first nothing happened, but then slowly the polar bear began to move.

As they started to lift off the ground, Emma wrapped her arms tight around the polar bear's neck.

And up they went!

They flew higher and higher—a girl,
a polar bear, and a cloud of brightly
colored balloons.

Emma pointed to her house, small and
glowing, as they drifted above it.

Farther and farther they went,
toward the North Star.

As the wind began to blow stronger and colder,
Emma snuggled her face into the polar bear's fur
until everything below disappeared.

They landed with a quiet thud.

Emma slid down his back, sinking into the snow.

She had never seen anything like it.

But before Emma could say anything, the polar bear set off north, his paws crunching with each step.

"Where are we going?" Emma asked as she trailed after him.

The polar bear was quiet.

They floated on icebergs, scaled icy mountains,
and trudged through knee-deep snow.

and Emma gazed with absolute wonder.

...vas a polar bear rumpus!

Emma was thankful she had
worn her boots.

Finally, they crept up over the last snowy hill . . .

and
danced.

It was after midnight when the sky
opened with snow, each flake lightly
kissing Emma's nose as it fell.

It had been a perfect adventure.

Emma and the polar bear
waved good-bye as the
iceberg slid into the night.

Emma slept on the polar bear's back as they floated home.

And didn't even wake up when
he tucked her into bed.

The next morning, Emma went to the carousel
to find everything as it always was.

No sign of any balloons.

GRAND
CAROUSEL

CLOSED

"Even if it wasn't real, it was the best adventure I've ever had," Emma whispered as she hugged the polar bear.

And there, tucked in his saddle was another note . . .